SUNSHINE

Tashi Chaturvedi

INDIA • SINGAPORE • MALAYSIA

ISBN 979-8-89277-229-7

I dedicate this book to my parents Mr Ajai Chaturvedi
and

Mrs Archana Chaturvedi

This book is a tribute to my grandparents Dr O.B.S. Chaubey and

Mrs Kalawati Chaturvedi

ACKNOWLEDGEMENTS

I am deeply grateful for the support and inspiration that made this book possible. Writing is a solitary endeavour, but the contributions of many have enriched this work.

I express my heartfelt gratitude to my mother for lending me her unwavering support and being there for me when I needed her the most. Her words 'I know you will do it' pushed me forward and fuelled my imagination every step of the way to write this book.

Mihir, my elder brother, who supported me throughout the writing process.

I extend sincere appreciation to my friends Dr Sumerah Waheed and Garima Srivastava whose valuable insights and constructive criticism helped me bring this story to life.

I cannot thank Anjum Sharfuddin enough for going through the manuscript and giving her invaluable suggestions.

The expertise of the team at Notion press was instrumental in making this book see the light of print.

Chapter 1

The day moves into evening and Anuj takes note of the time; it is 7.30 p.m. The whole day has been one meeting after another, and he is spent. He is a project leader at a multinational company and shoulders many responsibilities with stringent deadlines. In this job, he never has that awful Monday morning feeling. He loves his work but hates the stress and pressure that accompanies it. He decides to call it a day and shuts down his laptop, collects his stuff and puts it in the backpack. He pushes his chair out to stand up and sees Rohan come around. Rohan has a smiling face with a big broad-rimmed frame covering most part of his round profile. He is bald and keeps a perfectly trimmed French cut beard.

'Hi, Anuj. How are you doing'?

'Hi, Rohan. I am fine. Just wrapping up for the day. How about you'?

'I am good. I just finished a project and I am feeling great. I wanted to share some good news with you'.

'Oh really! What is it'?

'Well, you know how I have been working on that new app for the past few months, right'?

'Yes, I do. You have been very dedicated and passionate about it. I am impressed by your skills and creativity'.

'Thank you. That means a lot coming from you. You are an inspiration to me and many others. Anyway, the good news is that the app is finally ready and it is going to be launched tomorrow. And guess what? It has been selected as one of the featured apps on the app store. How cool is that'?

'Wow, that's amazing. Congratulations, Rohan. You have done a fantastic job. I am so happy for you. You deserve this success'.

'Thank you, Anuj. You are very kind. I could not have done it without your support and guidance. You have been a great mentor and friend to me. I owe you a lot'.

'No, no. You do not owe me anything. You have earned this on your own merit. You have a lot of talent and potential. I am proud of you'.

'Thank you, Anuj. You are too generous. I really appreciate it. Why don't we celebrate this occasion? Let us go out for dinner. What do you say'?

'Not today, the weather has gotten worse. Let us move fast'.

They turn on their heel and speed walk across the reception area to the basement parking lot where Rohan meets his team members and conversations ensue.

Anuj walks past them and catches snippets of their conversation: 'Manu has been removed from the project on account of...'

His swift sits at the far edge of the parking lot. He walks down to his car, climbs in, starts the ignition, and smoothly coasts it out on the main road. He switches on the stereo and soft Bollywood music pipes through the speakers. It helps him overcome stress and pulses him into deep relaxation.

By this time, black and grey clouds have rolled in and thunder rumbles in the distance. The sky flashes white with blasts of lightning. Large raindrops fall from the sky and the air carries the scent of damp earth. The street is deserted with no souls visible and no sounds audible. There is an irregular spacing between the streetlights, instead of the normal blanket covering. The moon is not even glowing tonight and there are few stars in the sky. He focuses on the road ahead and drives at a snail's pace through the rain soaked streets. Houses mark the street on both sides.

A small sound within earshot draws his attention. He slows down the car and pulls off to the side of the road. He sees a young woman sitting on a two-step stoop halfway down the street. Something about the situation does not seem right, so he stops and looks straight at the woman. She is clad in a long sleeves shirt and jeans that shields her from the monsoon wind. Her medium-length, honey coloured hair is slicked back into the perfect ponytail: not a flyaway to be seen. And then, he hears the sound that must have originally caught his attention.

Her shoulders convulse with sobs.

He experiences a stab of empathy but the thought of walking up to her sets off flutters in his stomach. He feels his hesitancy returning.

As soon as he restarts the car, her sobs grow louder and more insistent. He parks the car down the street, gets out, and walks on the narrow path lined by bushes with dark pink flowers, steadily covering the distance between them. He takes a deep breath to calm himself down. His stomach is tied in knots, but he finally clears his throat and manages to speak.

'Excuse me,' he says softly.

He tries to sound confident, but he is sure his voice has betrayed him. She looks up, startled at his approach, but then she slowly breathes in and out to collect herself. She scrunches up her face, as if searching for words.

'Are you okay?' He asks with an anxious frown.

She shoots him a look and he recognises the fight or flight expression on her face. But, soon enough, her apprehension melts to relief – and then to grief in hardly five seconds as she begins sobbing again.

She wipes her tears with the back of her hand and says, 'I am fine. Thank you for your concern.'

He notices that she is indeed young, pretty with no makeup.

Chapter 2

The young woman brings back memories of Sujata that sent wave of nostalgia through him.

Anuj had never expected to find love on Tinder, but when he saw Sujata's profile, he was instantly intrigued. She had a bright smile, and a shared interest in books and movies. He swiped right and hoped for the best. To his delight, he got a match notification soon after. He wasted no time in sending her a message, hoping to catch her attention. He complimented her on her choice of books and asked her what she was reading currently. Sujata replied within minutes, thanking him for his message and telling him that she was reading a thriller by Agatha Christie. She asked him if he liked mysteries and what his favourite genre was. Anuj was pleased by her response and quickly typed back that he loved mysteries and thrillers, especially by Sherlock Holmes and Dan Brown.

She also said that she liked science fiction and fantasy and mentioned some of her favourite books and shows in that genre. Anuj and Sujata found that they had a lot in common and conversation started flowing with ease. They exchanged opinions and recommendations, and steered clear of pretty much all things personal.

Sujata was a journalist who worked for a local newspaper.

Soon, their random chat blossomed into friendship, and he decided to ask her out for a cup of coffee.

It was time to put a face to the voice and text messages. He would get a better feel for her in person than from online, anyway.

He was nervous and excited, and hoped that she would say yes. He sent her a message, saying that he really enjoyed talking to her and wanted to meet her. He suggested a cosy café in the busy street of Chandni Chowk, not far from their workplace and asked her if she was free on Saturday afternoon.

Sujata was equally nervous and excited, and felt a flutter in her stomach. She liked Anuj a lot and wanted to see him face to face. She agreed to his invitation, saying that she was looking forward to meeting him and that the café sounded lovely. She also asked him to send her his phone number, so that they could call or text each other.

Anuj was overjoyed by her acceptance and sent her his number. He told her that he could not wait to see her and hear her voice. He also asked her to send him her number, so that he could save it in his phone. Sujata sent him her number.

She told him that she felt the same way and that she was counting the days until Saturday. They had found each other on Tinder, but they hoped that their relationship would last beyond the app.

Anuj was dressed to the nines: a blue shirt, black trousers and black shoes. His hair was neatly combed.

Fear and anxiety gripped him, and his head raced with different questions: 'What would I say when I met her?' 'How would I react?' 'What if she did not find me interesting enough?'

He had known that if he thought about it anymore, he would end up overthinking and cancelling on her. Thus he had arrived early, so there would be time to get his nerves under control. As he pulled into the parking space in front of the cafe, a family of five wandered by, talking and laughing as they did their best to catch drips from their ice cream cones.

The cafe was hidden from the public view; the canopy of bright foliage blocked the glare of the autumn sun. He pushed open the door and walked in. The interiors lend an earthy feel as it had unplastered rough-hewn walls.

He looked around the place, found a vacant table at a far right end corner and sat down. It appeared to be a couples' haven at first sight but gradually people of all age groups flocked the place. He began to beat the devil's tattoo on the wooden table with the fingers of his right hand. When he realised that it drew attention by the other customers present in the cafe, he stopped.

Minutes felt like hours.

Getting ready for the date proved to be more difficult than Sujata thought it would. She tried to pick something interesting and found the idea of wearing a black dress too boring. She finally decided on a pink top, a pair of navy blue trousers and stilettos.

Stupid to be nervous, she thought. It was just coffee. It was not a big deal.

She reached the cafe at 2.00 p.m. on the dot. She had worked herself up by the time she arrived. She resisted the urge to wipe her damp palms on the legs of her trousers. Taking a few deep breaths calmed down her otherwise agitated nerves and she felt better.

He stared at the carpet lost in thoughts when the noise of a chair being pulled out made him look up. A tall and slender girl with a pleasant countenance stood next to the chair. He stood up as a mark of courtesy, shook hands, exchanged greetings and the brunette slid into the seat across the table.

She had put on slight makeup. She was fair complexioned, her eyebrows were thick and beautifully arched, and her hazel eyes with long eyelids looked beautiful. She had a round, chubby face with a mole on her left cheek. Her nose was turned up at the tip and her well rounded fleshy lips were daubed in a light pink colour. Her hair was swept up into a sophisticated style. The fragrance of her perfume wafted through the air. The moment he set eyes on her, he knew he was in love.

Diverting himself from sinking into a bout of sadness over missing Sujata, he looks at the woman as her sobs return. He studies her face, looks for some sign of what she feels, but cannot get a read on her. He thinks she has love life troubles, after all. What else can a young, healthy, probably college girl has to cry about?

The area beyond the stoop is littered with tall trees and hanging creepers. The streetlamp bathes everything in an eerie glow. Occasionally, birds come and sit on the treetops. Silence fills the atmosphere except for the wind blowing through the trees. The gentle sound of the trees shaking in the breeze soothes him. There is room on the stoop, enough that he can sit beside her without getting uncomfortably close.

'May I sit here for a while?' He asks her with a hint of awkwardness.

She does not look his way but stiffens a fraction, just enough for him to notice because he is expecting this reaction.

He steps forward and eases his big frame onto the stoop. The concrete feels cool through his trousers.

'Is this okay?' He asks.

She glances at him quickly and relaxes, nodding slightly. She sighs now and then, but her tears have morphed to an occasional sniffle. He straightens up, and then rakes both hands through his hair. They sit quietly for a while, each lost in their own thoughts.

CHAPTER 3

Anuj has no idea what the young woman is thinking, but he is wondering why she is upset. Wondering why she has chosen this spot to sit and cry. Wondering how he would have felt about himself if he had opted to ignore her and just gone off home as he had countless evenings before this one. He knows he has helped even if he does not know anything about what has happened to her.

Then he notices two men walk by on the main street. One man glances towards them and hesitates – just a minor hitch in his stride. His face, not exactly pleasant in the first place, has twisted into an ugly mask of hostility. He has grey hair, his gut hanging out over his belt. He knows the man is assessing the situation: a guy sitting alone with a woman in a semi-hidden space. The man's forehead wrinkles up, as if he has had an important thought. Anuj guesses that he does a quick calculation in his mind, registering the fact that the guy seems to be in his early thirties, wearing a neat white shirt, black trousers, necktie, and employee ID badge clipped to his pocket. The woman appears to be there voluntarily, without being physically restrained, does not seem in immediate jeopardy. He knows that he would have followed the same thought pattern if he was seeing things from this man's perspective. The man looks away and walks on, immediately back in step with his companion.

Anuj figures he has not seen enough of a threat to feel the need to intervene at that moment. He glances at his watch and finds that twenty minutes have gone by.

The woman seems to have travelled from heavy sobbing to ordinary sadness in their quiet time together. He looks her square in the eye; there is intelligence in them with a hint of innocence, just like Sujata.

His thoughts drift to his coffee date with Sujata:

He says, 'You look gorgeous'.

She smiles and replies, 'Thanks, and you look handsome'.

He is thrilled to hear Sujata say those words.

'Thank you.'

She exclaims with a broad smile and then a grin, 'You look just like your picture on your tinder profile'.

'You too – calm and unassuming.'

He pauses to collect his thoughts.

'I want a picture of the two of us together in one frame.'

'Selfie'? She asks him.

'No, a proper picture.'

He looks around and goes up to a kind looking man sitting by himself. He asks him to click their picture and he agrees. They come towards her.

'He is Anurag Singh. He has agreed to take our photo.'

After clicking a few pictures, Anurag says, 'You make a lovely couple. Enjoy your trip'.

He then walks back to his table.

She looks up at Anuj with fiery eyes, 'You told that gentleman that we are on a trip'.

'Do not get angry Sujata. He was only willing to click the pictures after I said that.'

She folds her hands, sighs, and with a serious face says, 'I am learning another side of you I never knew before. I guess I could not see that side of you online'.

He puts both hands firmly on her shoulders and stares deep into her eyes.

'Forgive me Sujata. I was only trying to get our pictures clicked. You are safe with me.'

She looks at him in admiration. Trust is building up between them. He is calm and cool and handles everything with ease. He is smart and jaw-droppingly handsome too. What a man.

He asks her if she has a favourite sport, and she tells him she does not. She asks if he has and he tells her that his father pushed him to play hockey, but he fractured his wrist and had to quit.

She falls for him but finds ways to mask her feelings.

'What can I get you'? The waiter with blonde hair approaches their table and asks with a warm and inviting smile. He looks young, maybe nineteen or twenty at the most. The name tag pinned to his shirt reads 'Nitin'.

'Two espresso coffee with whipped cream.'

Nitin nods soberly.

'Accompaniments to go with it?'

'Chocolate chip cookies and potato wedges.'

'Sure.'

They smile at him as he takes the order and then cough nervously when he walks away.

She tells him about her trip to Jim Corbett National Park. He nods politely.

I have never met anyone like her before. I am obsessed with her. She is a picture of elegance.

The waiter returns with the order shortly.

They sip coffee and munch on cookies and wedges. She looks him in the eye and blushes. The moments blow past, and they let them. He swirls his fingers around the coffee mug and lets out a nervous chuckle. They make brief eye contact for the third time. She is beautiful with a warm smile, and he cannot take his eyes off her.

CHAPTER 4

He turns to her and says, 'I have a surprise for you today'.

She looks puzzled as he carries on, 'We will do some shopping this evening'.

'You know I am a shopaholic. You will need your strength to keep up with me', she says laughing.

They finish coffee, settle the bill and exit the cafe. He tells her to wait while he goes and gets his car from the parking area. He is back within minutes; she gets in and they head towards downtown market. One lane is closed due to construction and the vehicles move slowly. The lights turn red. He waits for the traffic lights to open.

Life seems much better when we share it with someone.

They do not interact much but enjoy each other's company. He pulls over in front of the market and parks underneath a billboard sign, surprised that what turned out to be a forty-five minute drive has passed so quickly. It is a shopper's paradise. Sujata is fascinated by the lovely clothing in the shops. She wants to try on every dress she sees in the display window but resists the temptation for the fear of boring him. They buy a few personal items and relax in an ice cream shop for a while; thereafter, they decide to return to their respective homes and rest.

On their way back, Anuj wants to tell her that he loves her but instead blurts out, 'Sujata, someday I will cook you a lovely dinner'.

'Can you cook'? She asks.

'Sure, I can cook any dish.'

He brings the car to a halt in front of her apartment complex and his heart races with anticipation. He is suddenly lost for words. He sneaks a look to see if she is watching. Her piercing eyes are fixed on him. His right hand slowly moves to take her left hand. She does not object. He feels the warmth of her hands and longs to take her in his arms. Not yet, he thinks. It has taken them months of friendship and countless conversations to reach this point, and Anuj does not want to rush things. They embrace each other and then slowly release their hold.

If we are lucky, tomorrow will be much the same. These are the best of days and I never want them to change.

She waves and smiles as she bids him good night. With a sigh, he drives homewards. It is late when he reaches the apartment. He unbolts the door, enters and goes to his room, his tread soundless so that he does not wake up dad.

The morning sun wakes him up and he feels the calm of a decision made. Their friendship has evolved into something beautiful and he decides to let it flourish, one day at a time. He jumps from the bed as fast as his body will allow, climbs into the shower and gets ready, gathers his car keys and leaves for office. As he starts the engine and merges into the morning traffic, he cannot shake off the smile that has been on his face since he woke up.

The drive to the office passes in a blur and he arrives at the workplace, his professional demeanour intact. He has got a lot of work to do, but he cannot get down to it. He had never had such strong feelings for anyone and is anxious to call her and hear her voice. Finally, he takes out his phone and punches her number, a strange voice answers.

He thinks he has dialled the wrong number, so he disconnects and tries Sujata's number again.

The same voice is at the other end.

'Are you trying to call Sujata'? The male voice answers. 'If you know her, then please come to the hospital morgue and identify her body'.

'What', Anuj yells into the phone.

His heart skips a few beats. He can feel his heart pounding in his chest like a hammer.

'Your friend died today. Her body is in the morgue.'

'No. No. I do not believe that.'

He asks, 'Who are you'?

The man replies, 'I am a police officer. I am at the morgue. Sujata died in a road accident. Are you a relative'?

'We are close friends', he replies.

'Can you come in to identify the body?'

'Sure. I will be there by 8.30 p.m.'

He finds it hard to focus and it is not until evening that he manages to complete the day's work.

He realises that every breath is precious and every minute they spend on Earth is a blessing. How much are we attached to life when it is too late? How many days have we wasted and how many lives are cut short for no reason?

He tosses these questions but finds no answers. His mind finally goes numb, and he is unable to think anymore.

He checks the time; it is 7.00 p.m. He touches his forehead to calm a headache and leaves the office premises for the hospital morgue. He still cannot believe that Sujata has gone. He thinks about it through the entire drive, and it makes his heart bleed.

Upon his arrival, he is met by the police officer who introduces himself as 'Dheeraj Sharma'. He is a middle-aged skinny man, freshly shaved with light hair that needs a trim. After checking the identification, he takes him to the morgue, asks him if he is ready and lifts the sheet covering Sujata.

Shock spreads through his whole body. His legs cannot hold him anymore. He lets himself drop to the ground, hugs his knees to his chest and holds himself in a tight embrace while long sobs shake his body. His brain cannot find any words and his mouth is too dry to say them anyway. He wants to get into his car more than anything, but he has not moved an inch.

The police officer interrupts and asks if everything is all right. He nods and asks him to give him a few minutes to calm down. Then he leaves the hospital.

CHAPTER 5

'My dad died this morning', the woman says, jolting Anuj from his thoughts, her voice cracking as it edges into the silent night. Her words hang heavily in the air. Anuj's heart sinks, empathising with the pain in her voice. He feels a sudden urge to reach out, to offer comfort in any way he can. He can see the weight of her sorrow etched on her face as if a storm has swept through her life, leaving her broken and vulnerable.

The woman takes a deep breath and carries on, her voice quivering with every word.

'My mom just called. Hit by a motorbike while returning from work.'

Anuj feels a lump forming in his throat as he listens to her devastating revelation. He cannot fathom the pain she must be experiencing. In that moment, Anuj knows he has to be there for her, to provide solace and support. He gently places a hand on her trembling shoulder, offering a small gesture of comfort.

'Oh, dear', he says 'I am so sorry'.

'Thanks', she says.

He knows what it is like to lose someone you love. Anuj realises that mere words will not be enough to heal her wounds, but perhaps the presence of a compassionate stranger can offer a glimmer of hope.

He has one of those dismissive quips ready, like 'do not have any choice', but he holds back.

As the night wears on, their conversation ebbs and flows, an exchange of sorrow and hope. Anuj listens patiently, offering words of comfort when needed and simply being a compassionate presence when silence seems more appropriate.

'I am okay now. I have to make some calls. Get a flight home'. She adds, 'Life is very unpredictable. Never take things for granted. Express love for each other always. Do not let minor incidents spoil relationships. Do not live with regrets. Living with regret is far worse than living with fear'.

She speaks so slowly it hurts his ears to listen.

A jumble of questions swirl inside his mind: Is just being there for a fellow human being sometimes enough? Just offering silent company in a time of need? Will it bring her a sliver of comfort?

The young woman gets up and turns, climbs the steps, and uses a key card to open the door. She smiles at him softly as she passes by his side: a soft, benign smile. She is slim, svelte and sophisticated. Anuj realises that she lives here. He is on her front step, a guest who has invited himself into her home.

She flicks her hand through her hair, turns and catches the door before it swings close. She looks back at him, her face level with his, maybe even a few inches higher because she stands atop the steps. Again, she uses several minutes to thank him. Her voice contains trace amounts of anxiety, and her brown eyes cannot disguise her stress. She turns and hurries through the glass door as it closes behind her.

He can see her sneakered feet moving upward and fading into the shadows as she climbs the stairs inside. She will move forward as she moves up those stairs and out of sight, gone from his life. After a few seconds, all he can see in the glass door is his own reflection.

Life always goes on, but often I think it should not. I see hundreds of people every day, walking around like nothing has happened, like nothing has changed.

The veil of darkness has finally lifted and the clouds cloaking the moon are swept away on the breeze.

He retreats to his car and drives through the virtually empty street towards home, once again.

If only I had gathered courage to express my feelings to Sujata the very same day...

He is overwhelmed with thoughts when a sudden jerk hurtles him back to the present.

The car stops. He tries to start it but to no avail.

'Oh No! My car is on the fritz.'

He gets down and looks out for cabs but does not spot any. He is in a fix. Just then, a man comes up to him and asks if he needs a cab. Anuj nods, leaves his car there and follows the man to the car parked on the opposite side of the street. He tells the man his home address and the man drives off. It is dark and Anuj is not able to see much outside.

In the meantime, he observes the driver closely. He wears shoulder-length auburn hair and has light brown eyes. A long snake is tattooed on his left arm. After about thirty minutes, he becomes restless and asks the driver if they are there.

'In five minutes', he says.

Anuj becomes suspicious and looks around the vehicle for a registration number but finds none. Suddenly, the brake slams and he jolts in his seat. The driver comes out and opens the door to the passenger seat. He gets out and looks around. The place is secluded and very few pedestrians comb the street.

'What is this place'? He asks.

'Pass me your cell phone, wallet and wristwatch.'

Anuj is shocked and scared. He tries to reason with the driver, but the driver with a gap in his teeth says as he points a gun at him, 'Just pass your things if you do not want to get hurt'. He hands over his belongings to the driver. He takes them and drives away.

Anuj is left stranded on the road. At that moment he regrets not asking him for his name and proper credentials before boarding his car, but it is too late to think about all this now. He realises that he is not very far from home – right turn from the roundabout and another hundred metres from there. He must make the best of his way home. A walk through the darkness seems to last hours, but it is only fifteen minutes. Finally, he finds himself on the ground floor of his apartment complex.

CHAPTER 6

Anuj steps into the elevator and presses the button to the third floor. As soon as the elevator door opens, he hears a scream so loud that he is sure plaster is cracking and glasses are breaking somewhere. He recognises the voice as that of his dad. He runs like greased lightning to the apartment door and rings the doorbell multiple times in a state of panic. He hears footsteps approaching and the unclasping of the latch.

The door opens and Amar stands there. He moves to one side and gives space to Anuj to go inside. He walks briskly to dad's room, which is to the right of the kitchen. Dad is breathing heavily from exhaustion.

'Dad, are you okay'? Anuj asks, rushing to his side.

He rubs his knees and winces in pain from a knee jerk.

After a while, he fills him in: 'I held the arm of the wheelchair with my left hand and tried to sit on the bed after I came back from the washroom, in the process I lost balance and landed on the floor. It was Kittu who saw me fall and rushed to Amar's room and got him here in time'.

'Yes, she clawed at my door and yowled incessantly until I opened it and got me here', Amar added.

Amar is a young manservant who lived on the alms basket before dad brought him into the house. He stays at dad's elbow, in case he needs help.

He stares at Kittu with affection, and she butts her head into him.

Dad was in his prime when a car accident left him wheelchair-bound: t-boned at an intersection. He had a lucrative job at the petroleum refinery but downgraded to the job of a home tutor to cover all expenses. He found the courage to start over when life threw us a curve.

Dad bids him goodnight and he goes to his room with Kittu in tow; he is all in. He switches on the night bulb and a soft glow radiates out into the room. He quickly changes into T-shirt and lounge pants, lies down on his bed and pulls the blanket over his head to protect himself from insects. Kittu wraps herself into a ball in her grey carrier bed placed at the right-hand corner of the room.

His mind wanders to the thoughts of his mom who was called to her last account when he was an infant in arms. She was aware of the complications involved in her pregnancy but there was so much enthusiasm and excitement about it that she decided to forgo doctor's advice.

'Giving birth to a baby can be life-threatening for you', the doctor said.

She did not even tell dad about this in a bid not to hurt his feelings.

Sometimes things are nice and sad all at once.

As he listens to Kittu's gentle purring, he feels better. He first encountered Kittu on a Friday evening in November. The lift in the apartment block was not working, so he headed for the first flight of stairs, resigned to make the long trudge up to the third floor. The strip lighting in the hallway was broken and part of the ground floor was swathed in darkness, but as he made his way to the staircase, he could not help noticing a pair of glowing eyes in the dark. Edging closer, in the half-light, he could see a kitten curled up outside one of the ground-floor flats in the corridor that led off the hallway. He had not seen her around the flats before, but she looked like she was very much at home there in the shadows. He was drawn to the cat's sweet little face with the terracotta nose outlined in pink. Her yellow eyes were completely captivating. She brushed herself lightly against him and gently rubbed her face against his feet with little flattering noises. She was purring away, appreciating the attention she was getting. She rode the stairs alongside him, and he could not help wondering about her story: where she had come from and what sort of life she had led before she had come and sat on the mat downstairs. Part of him was convinced that she was a family pet. She was a fine-looking cat.

She must really trust me, he thought to himself.

Upon entering the apartment, she headed for the living room where she curled up on the floor, close to the chair where dad sat. He told dad how he found her, fished out some milk from the fridge and poured it into a saucer. She lapped it up in seconds. Again, he gave the cat a bowl of mashed biscuits and milk and again, she wolfed it down. Poor thing, she must be absolutely starving.

'She needs a name', dad said.

'Kittu.'

'Yes, that suits her perfectly.'

He felt like he had an extra purpose in his life, something positive to do for someone or something, other than himself.

CHAPTER 7

Gradually his eyelids droop and he drops off into a dreamless sleep until his consciousness is stirred by a pounding on the main door. He spots the time on the digital clock beside the bed. It is 6.30 a.m, the time when the milkman arrives with the milk can. His punctuality cannot be questioned upon.

Kittu is asleep in her carrier bed. A bowl filled with cat food is kept near it along with a water bowl.

He blinks a few times to clear away the sleep. He rolls on his back, pushes the covers aside, and gets up lazily. Sun shines through the glass windowpanes that cover the east wall. It is comfortably warm. He slips his feet into a pair of flip flops, walks up to the main door, and opens the deadbolt. He is greeted by the milkman's never waning smile. He pours milk in the plastic container and leaves. Anuj closes the door.

He has to reach office by 8.30 a.m. It is already 6.50 a.m. He quickly tidies up his room: makes the bed, organises the stuff kept on his bedside table, and arranges his clothes in a neat pile and puts them in the closet adjacent to the foot of the bed.

Everything must be in apple-pie order. It is bred in his bone.

The sound of moving utensils on the cabinet and the flick of a lighter tells him that dad is in the kitchen. He is in the habit of keeping good hours. He is an excellent cook, a connoisseur of food and has brought his long-lost passion to life. He is in his element there. The kitchen opens out into the dining room.

A smile lights up his face. He takes out clothes from the closet – a white shirt and blue trousers – then steps into the shower.

'Breakfast is ready, come soon, lest it turns cold', dad's voice reaches his ears.

Amar helps dad set the table.

He quickly slips his feet into formal black shoes, grabs his cell phone and backpack, switches off the fan and is out of the door.

'What is for breakfast, dad'? He asks.

'Cheese mushroom sandwich, scrambled eggs and apple juice.'

I love mushroom sandwich so much that I can polish off four in a row.

The round four seater glass dining table occupies the centre of the room with chairs around it. Anuj pulls a chair out and sits down with the platter in front of him while dad sits across from him with the newspaper. As he washes down the cheese sandwich with apple juice, his gaze falls on the advertisement that reads:

'A new revolution in medical science – a team of doctors from Apollo Hospital has successfully operated upon a woman who had suffered spine injury in a road accident.'

Same case as that of his dad.

Anuj feels a surge of hope as he reads the advertisement. He wonders if this can be the answer to his dad's problem. Dad has given up on his dream of travelling the world.

He decides to find out more about the operation. He finds the contact details given at the bottom of the advertisement and calls the hospital. He is connected to a receptionist who asks him what he wants. He tells her he wants to know more about the spine surgery that is advertised in the newspaper. She transfers him to a doctor who introduces herself as Dr Agarwal. She asks Anuj what he wants to know.

Anuj tells her about his dad's condition and asks her if he is eligible for the surgery. Dr Agarwal says she needs to see his dad's medical reports and examine him personally before she can say anything. She asks Anuj to bring his dad to the hospital for a consultation and further adds that the surgery is very expensive and risky, but it has a high success rate.

It can change his dad's life.

Anuj is excited and nervous. He thanks Dr Agarwal and hangs up. He runs to his dad and tells him the news. He tells dad to read the advertisement. He requests him to go to the hospital and try the surgery. He says it can be their last chance.

His dad is sceptical and scared. He says he does not want to waste money and time on something that may not work. He does not want to get his hopes up and be disappointed.

Anuj tries to convince him. He says he has faith in the doctors and the technology. He has seen the testimonials of the patients who have undergone the surgery and recovered. He says he has saved enough money from his job to pay for the surgery.

His dad is touched by his words and actions. His face expression changes from sombre to that of hope and excitement.

They decide to fix an appointment with the doctors.

Amar clears the table and Anuj tells him to take his car to the mechanic and get it repaired. He picks up his things, bids goodbye to dad and rushes out of doors. Kittu follows him and sees him go. The cab waits at the entrance gate of the complex; he slides into the backseat of the waiting car and gives the office address to the driver.

The day progresses and meetings take up most part of it. Anuj packs his things and swipes his card at the door to push it open. He steps into the lobby, crosses its length, and is out of the office premises. He hires a cab and leaves for home.

On reaching the apartment, he sees Kittu waiting for him at the front door. She follows him to the living room and curls up at his feet as he sinks into the armchair opposite to the couch with a glass of water. She bears him company. A blue striped hanging rug covers the wall behind the couch which is in complete contrast to the wall paint. He keeps his backpack on the wooden centre table and dad looks up with a smile. Dad is propped up on the couch reading a book on the history of Rome, sipping on his cup of coffee. Anuj rests his head on his folded arms, hoping to give his eyes a short break. He wakes up some time later and stretches.

Forty winks on the chair was not a good idea.

CHAPTER 8

*O*h! *I just forgot. I have to call the hospital and take an appointment.*

He goes to the rack, placed close to the left end of the wall in the passage that leads to the living room, and pulls out today's newspaper from the stack of newspapers.

He rings up the hospital and a lady answers the call.

'Hello, Apollo Hospital.'

'Hi! I am Anuj Sharma and I want an appointment in the orthopedic department for tomorrow morning for my father. He suffers from spine-related medical condition.'

The lady checks the availability of the orthopedic doctors and says, 'Mr Sharma, we have a slot for tomorrow at 10.30 a.m. with Dr Agarwal. She is one of the best spine surgeons in the country. Would you like to book it?'

Anuj feels a surge of relief and hope.

'Yes, please. Thank you so much.'

The lady replies, 'Thank you! Have a good day'.

He hangs up.

Tomorrow is Sunday, so no office.

He goes to his dad's room and says, 'I have good news for you. I have booked an appointment with Dr Agarwal at Apollo hospital for tomorrow morning'.

His dad looks at him with gratitude and a little grin creeps up on his face, 'Thank you son. I am so proud of you'.

Anuj hugs his dad and says, 'Do not worry dad, everything will be fine. We will go together tomorrow and see what he says'.

They have a relaxing dinner, and he switches on the music player kept on the mantel placed at right angle to the door. Twenty minutes gone and they are done. Dad bids him goodnight and retires to bed.

He goes to his room and Kittu comes in from behind and literally trips him. He takes bedstand's support to prevent the fall. He grabs a quick shower before going to bed, shuts his eyes, and washes away all the dust and sweat of the day. He climbs into bed and eases his head down on the pillow while Kittu hops into her carrier bed. Moonlight pools in through the gap in the curtains. He goes from being completely asleep to fully awake with no transition in between.

It is 7.30 a.m. The sun is high and bright, casting easy shadows on the balcony. They throw themselves into their routine and are ready by 9.30 a.m. Dad has slathered butter on the toast. They quickly wash it down with cups of coffee and exit through the main door to go to the hospital. Amar wheels dad out and bolts the door.

Anuj takes the keys and walks briskly to the car. He turns on the ignition and within minutes, they are on the way to the hospital. The commute to the hospital is less than thirty minutes, but it feels like eternity for Anuj. He is anxious and nervous about his dad's condition and the outcome of the consultation. He tries to calm himself by listening to some music and chatting with dad. Dad is also nervous but he tries to hide it from him. He knows how much Anuj has sacrificed for him and how hard he has worked to get this appointment. He does not want to disappoint him or let him down. He hopes that Dr Agarwal will have some good news for him and that he will be able to walk again. They reach the hospital and park the car in the basement.

Many mature oak trees grace the property. The potted plants surrounding the patio are ablaze with colour. Amar helps dad get out of the car and assists him to the hospital's reception desk. Anuj follows. He can smell the sweet scent of the flowers.

A lady with a pleasing personality stands behind the front desk. She smiles brightly at him.

'Hi! I am Anuj Sharma. I have an appointment with the doctor in the orthopedic department.'

She says, 'Welcome Mr Sharma. You are right on time. Dr Agarwal is waiting for you in room number 12. Please follow me'.

She leads them to a spacious and well-equipped room, where Dr Agarwal is sitting behind a large oak table with a computer and some files. When she looks up at Anuj from behind the pile of papers sprawled on the table, he immediately recognises her. She is the same woman whom he met midway while returning from work. She passes him a smile and he reciprocates the same.

The plaque on her table reads 'Dr Shikha Agarwal'. She looks up and greets them warmly.

'Hello, Mr Sharma. I am Dr Agarwal, your spine surgeon. Please have a seat and make yourself comfortable.'

She invites them to sit on two chairs facing her and asks them some basic questions about their medical history, symptoms, medications and lifestyle. She then examines dad's spine to check his reflexes, muscle strength and sensation. She gets a spine x-ray done and asks them to wait for sometime while she reviews the results on her computer. They look at each other with anticipation and apprehension. They wonder what Dr Agarwal will say and what she will recommend.

A framed picture of Dr Agarwal with her mother is kept on the table. Seeing it, he calls to mind a memory and the joyful part of it fills his mind.

Sujata had posted a picture of her mother with the caption 'You mean so much to me that distance does not matter'.

He commented on it, 'May she rest in peace'.

The very next moment, his phone rings. He checks the screen. It is a call from Sujata. His eyes shine and a real, genuine smile draws on his face.

He picks up on the first ring and she bursts out, 'Read the caption carefully. We reside in different cities. My mother is in perfect health. Delete the comment at once, else condolence messages will begin to pour in'.

He covers his mouth and laughs silently.

'Sorry Sujata. I misunderstood it', he says and hangs up.

He deletes the comment and laughs out loud.

Dr Agarwal looks up with a smile on her face and says, 'Mr Sharma, I have some good news for you. Your spinal disorder is not as severe as we thought. It is caused by a herniated disc in your lower back that is pressing on your spinal cord and nerves. It can be treated with surgery'. She shows them images of his spine on her computer screen and explains the procedure in detail.

She says, 'The surgery is very safe and effective. It takes about an hour and you can go home in a few days. You will have to wear a brace for a few weeks and do some physiotherapy exercises to strengthen your back muscles and improve your mobility. You should be able to restore your normal activities within a month or two'.

She adds, 'The success rate of this surgery is very high, more than ninety per cent. Most patients experience significant improvement in their pain and function after the surgery'.

She looks at them with confidence and compassion and says, 'Mr Sharma, I am sure that this surgery will help you recover from your spinal disorder and restore your quality of life'.

Dad is speechless with joy. He cannot believe what he has just heard. He feels like he has been given a new lease of life.

He looks at Anuj with tears in his eyes and says, 'Our bleak days have gained new hope. Yesterday the answer was a firm no, now it is a pliable maybe'.

A thrilling jolt of energy rushes through him at the thought of seeing dad walk again. He says, 'This is the best news ever. I am so happy for you.'

'What will be the total cost involved?' Anuj asks anxiously.

'The total cost will come to around 10 – 12 lakh', she replies with a grave expression.

He looks up at dad and sees tears of joy prick his eyes. He blinks them away. He has always admired dad's resilience and unwavering support.

She says, 'The surgery will be done next week on Monday at 9.00 a.m. and gives them some instructions about the preparation, recovery, follow-up etc.'

She hands them some papers with more details and says, 'Please read these carefully and sign them if you agree to proceed with the surgery'.

Dad nods eagerly and signs the papers without hesitation.

Dr Agarwal says, 'Great! You are all set then. I will see you next week on Monday. Please call me if you have any questions or concerns before the surgery'.

She shakes their hands and wishes them good luck.

Anuj and his dad thank her again and leave the room with a smile on their faces. Amar wheels dad out of the hospital premises.

They get into the car and drive back home, dreaming of a better future.

CHAPTER 9

En route to home, Anuj's smile drops away and gravity takes over the corners of his lips. The estimated cost of 10 −12 lakh for surgery has toned down their usually jovial car rides. He knows he cannot manage it on his own. He casts about how he will arrange the funds when dad nudges him on the shoulder. Anuj turns to face his dad with a touch of concern. Dad reads between the lines and tells him that he will encash his fixed deposits, saved for the rainy day, and arrange approximately five lakh. He can see dad bottle up his emotions. He is a man of few words; his face speaks volumes, but he says nothing.

Dad's support and sacrifice touches him deeply. In that moment, he realises that the true cost of the surgery is not only in terms of money, but also it is a measure of the love that binds them together. Their shared determination to deal with this financial challenge brings them closer than ever.

Rest of the distance is covered in silence, but a comforting one.

Upon reaching the apartment, he fumbles for the keys and unlocks the door. He pushes it open, and dad goes in with Amar. The heat of the day has left them exhausted. Amar switches on the fan and takes out a water bottle from the refrigerator. Dad makes a long arm for the glasses kept on the cabinet, next to the couch. Amar pours water into the glasses, and they drain it in seconds.

Anuj goes to his room to change and lies on the bed; his head is popped up on pillows, eyes closed, and he reflects on everything that has happened today.

'For dad's surgery, I will take out my savings that will come around to three lakh. Further, my promotion is in the offing as per the company policy and my performance scorecard.'

The rest of the day unfolds as a blend of routine and leisure activities.

The sun bathes their living room in a warm, golden glow as they wrap up the usual weekend chores.

Anuj sorts through a pile of laundry, expertly separating colours from whites, and soon the washing machine hums with efficiency. Dad, a stickler for neatness, takes charge of arranging the closets with Amar in tow. The sound of hangars sliding across the metal rod is accompanied by a sense of order being restored in their lives.

However, the highlight of the day is the unfinished glass painting. He had started working on a beautiful glass design weeks ago. He has always been a dab hand with a paint brush. His creative side comes to the fore when he picks up a set of vibrant glass paints. The play of colours on the transparent canvas intrigues him.

As they sit together side by side at the table, dad occasionally offers subtle suggestions and he puts finishing touches on the glass painting. This accomplishment transcends the financial concern that earlier weighed on their mind.

Dad and Amar prepare a simple dinner and its comforting aroma fills the kitchen. They quickly finish dinner and call it an early night. It has been a very long day and he is worn to the frazzle.

As Anuj drifts into slumber, he cannot help but feel grateful for the simple joys of the day.

Monday morning arrives with its regular hustle and bustle. Anuj has an early start and he meets dad at the dining table, set for breakfast of omelette with toast, cornflakes and yoghurt. This omelette with diced radishes is his favourite. It is very delicious.

They sit down together, exchanging light morning conversation as they enjoy their breakfast. After they finish the meal, Anuj picks up his bag and leaves for office. Dad sees him off with a reassuring nod. He gets in the car, turns the key in the ignition and the engine starts up. He pulls it out on the main road. It takes forty minutes to reach office due to heavy flow of traffic.

He is already thirty minutes late. Upon entering the office premises, he makes a beeline for his workstation, acknowledging his colleagues with apologetic smiles and hurried nods. He has a lot to catch up on, and without wasting time he dives into his tasks: emails await attention, reports need review, and meetings have been scheduled. It is going to be a busy day and he is determined to make up for the lost time. As the morning moves into afternoon, Anuj's focus remains unwavering. He plows through the tasks with remarkable efficiency and meets his deadlines. His fingers dance across the keyboard, and his analytical mind solves problems and makes decisions with precision. The day draws to a close and Anuj has not only caught up on his work but also has made significant progress on other pending projects. The knot of anxiety that had gripped him upon arriving late has transformed into a sense of accomplishment and relief. He logs off his computer and leaves for the day.

The air is still and hot but beginning to cool for the night. It is almost 8.00 p.m. when he reaches home and the scorching heat of the day still clings like a heavy, wet towel steaming hot, draped over him. Kittu is lying in her bed with her eyes closed. As soon as he opens the door, her eyes pop open and she hops off her bed and rubs her face on his feet. He picks her up and makes her sit on his lap. The day has been a whirlwind of tasks, meetings, and deadlines and the weight of responsibility pressed upon him. Her soft and gentle purring makes him let go of all the stress and tension of the day. After around fifteen minutes, she jumps down and delves into her food bowl.

The warm, welcoming glow of the lights in the living room lends it a soft ambience. Dad smiles as he enters. The aroma of a home cooked meal wafts from the kitchen.

'Dinner is ready', dad says.

He goes to the washroom with the change. Table is set by the time he comes into the dining room. They savour the flavours of the meal in conversing about the events of the day to their dreams and hopes for their future. Dinner concludes and it is time to call it a night. They retire to their respective rooms for peaceful sleep.

In the morning, Anuj puts the tea kettle on to boil and lets it steep for several minutes. He pours tea into two cups and brings it to the table. As usual, dad sits with his newspaper. With the boost of caffeine, his morning ritual kicks into high gear and within one hour and thirty minutes, he is at his desk in office. The first unread email catches his attention. It is from the human resource department. He clicks on it and the email opens. He goes over it slowly and takes in each word with difficulty. The email drops the bombshell.

It reads: 'You have been moved to the operations department as assistant manager with immediate effect. Your promotion has been stalled for one year'.

This gets his back up. Just two lines, but enough to make his life – the good life he is so proud of – crumble around him. He has worked his tail off to climb the corporate ladder.

I am at my wit's end. It seems that I am being plunged into a network of fresh difficulties.

Rohan sees him at his desk and comes over. He is formally dressed in a starched white shirt complemented with a black blazer, grey trousers and black shoes.

Anuj shows him the email. His forehead wrinkles up as he reads it. Rohan tells him to discuss it with his immediate boss, the regional head Mr Rishabh Saxena.

Rohan is soft-spoken and has the habit of dispensing advice, unwanted at times. His advice generally ranges from what kind of gas to put in the car to where to invest money and how much. Although unsolicited, his advice is mostly sincere and always has his friend's best interest in mind. He is the first person Anuj turns to whenever life wears him down. He gives ears to his problems and his voice washes over him like that of a reassuring friend. Anuj looks away for a minute to give himself time to organise his thoughts.

He switches off the monitor and goes to meet Mr Rishabh Saxena. He is not in his cabin. Anuj takes out his cell phone and dials his number, but the call goes unanswered. Almost instantly, his phone dinges with a text from Mr Saxena:

'I am out of station today and will resume work tomorrow.'

CHAPTER 10

Anuj reaches home in the late evening hours and looks down in the mouth. He goes to his room and does not come down even for dinner. His loud sobs cut dad to the bone and Amar pushes his wheelchair and brings him to the door of the room. He tries to open the door, but it is bolted from inside, so he knocks wildly on it.

The door opens and he stands there, eyes red, and tears spill down his cheeks. He flings himself in dad's arms and dissolves into tears.

He tells him about the email, all in a breath.

Wiping his tears, dad says, 'Pull yourself together! You must face up to your problems. You just need to believe in yourself'.

I always count on dad to set my heart at rest when I am racked with anxiety.

All the negativity inside him melts away, replaced by a warm smile he cannot suppress. Kittu walks across his lap, turns around and settles down. 'Meow! Meow! Meow'! is her constant banter.

They need us and the occasional moments of kindness we offer.

The very look of her honest face makes him forget all the cares of the day. Her soft caresses soothe him. He lifts Kittu off him and puts her down on the floor. They go down together for dinner and sit around the dining table. Dad has prepared mixed vegetables and rice. Its tantalizing aroma makes his mouth water. Amar serves the meal in their plates, and they begin to eat.

During the course of the meal, dad tells Anuj, 'The surgery is proposed for tomorrow morning'.

'Yes dad. I am with you every step of the way.'

Anuj looks up at him with a sparkle of hope in his eye. Dad beams with a wide, affectionate smile.

They finish dinner in silence and go to their rooms.

The next day, they arrive early at the hospital for preoperative procedures. He is a little disoriented and accidentally rams into Dr Agarwal in the corridor.

She smiles and says in her most reassuring tone, 'Stay calm, everything is going to be fine'.

'Thank you', he adds 'I have not made the payment in full. I will drum up the remaining funds by tomorrow'.

She continues to smile warmly.

'It has been taken care of', she says, contentment etched on her face, as she reaches out and gently touches both his forearms.

He raises an eyebrow, unable to respond, but he is sure the answer is written all over his face. She is not short of the milk of human kindness.

Many a time, you realise how priceless a moment is only when it becomes a memory. Always remember people who helped you out in distressed times. You share your story with them who have earned the right to hear it out.

He sees dad being wheeled into the operation theatre. Dad waves to him with optimistic eyes and a smile pasted on his face.

He looks after her as she goes inside the operation theatre and the door panels fall in place.

I experience at first hand the miracle of chance encounters.

He sits in the waiting room along with Amar. His anxiety is palpable. Time drags on and finally, Dr Agarwal emerges from the operation theatre with a reassuring smile. The surgery has gone well but the road to recovery will be challenging.

He walks up to his car, climbs in, and drives off to office.

Thick traffic makes driving a wearisome task. He reaches office and goes through the emails in his mailbox. The desk phone rings, and the call is from Mr Saxena:

'Hello, good afternoon sir', he says.

'Good Afternoon, Anuj. Please come to my cabin', Mr Saxena says and hangs up.

His hands flow upward in quick movements to smooth and tweak his back combed hair. All his joints are dripping with tension and anxiety. He knocks on the door and pushes it open with little effort.

Mr Saxena sits at the head of the rectangular table. He goes inside and takes a seat.

Mr Saxena is a man in his early fifties. His sharp features give him a serious look, like a man to contend with; but when he smiles, his face softens into a friendly surprise. He wears mild cologne, and its smell is soothing to the senses.

'Sir, did you go through the email that talks about my department and designation change along with stalled promotion for another year?'

I do not like the way I have worded my question, but that is the best I can do at the moment. I am on the anxious seat.

'Yes, this is the management's decision, and my hands are tied', he says staring him straight in the eyes.

His demeanour has a hint of arrogance to it.

Anuj manages to keep his countenance through the meeting. His hopes fall to the ground. He gets up and leaves the cabin. He feels weak and helpless, and his eyes start to tear up. He wants to cry but holds it in. He steps into the parking area and the hot sun enervates him to the point of collapse.

He leaves for the hospital to see dad and relays everything to him who encourages him to keep his head: 'If one thing does not fly, you need to try something else until you discover something that works'.

His words manage to sink in and are etched somewhere in his consciousness. Seeing how well dad has handled everything till now keeps him from breaking down.

He gets into the car and heads back home. He realises he has not eaten in almost a day, but with all the stress and anxiety, he has forgotten all about food. The minutes crawl by and become hours and he looks out of his room window at the sun that quickly sets in the horizon. He is mesmerised by the perfectly shaped orange circle. He must have forgotten how beautiful sunsets can be and how much they fail to appreciate the simple, beautiful things. The sky grows darker and is embellished with stars. The fire alarm blares through the house. He drops his cell phone on the bed and rushes to the kitchen, where smoke pours from the oven and Kittu cowers under the table. He slips his hands into the oven mittens and pulls the tray out of the oven. He reaches for the broom and taps the alarm. Its siren continues, so he hits it hard a second time and the alarm finally stops. Kittu creeps from under the table and gives him a tired look as if blaming him for disturbing her sleep. She circles around his legs, seeks comfort and he strokes her neck to calm her. He tosses the withered, shrunken potatoes in the garbage and feels an urge to scream. This is the first time he has burned anything in two decades. He blames himself for being so absent-minded. He opens the door to air out the house.

Chapter 11

Kittu rubs against his legs again; he picks her up and she curls into his arms. He strokes her ears, and she starts to purr.

The evening goes by like the turn of a page. He eats badly and turns in for the night. His eyelids feel heavy, but he does not want to close his eyes, wondering whether the following day will bring forth any positive news.

Anuj wakes up from a fitful sleep and the bright light coming through the window lets him know it is well into morning. He jumps off the bed and looks at the time. It is 7.45 a.m. He hurries through the morning routine, has a quick breakfast and leaves for the hospital.

Daily, Anuj visits his father and watches him as he starts his rehabilitation, slowly regaining strength and mobility.

In office, he is busy the whole day with meetings and calls. He stands outside Mr Saxena's cabin when four fifty rolls around. The clock above the door ticks its seconds. He is torn between hope and despair.

'Mr Saxena, may I come in'? He asks after softly knocking on the door.

A voice answers from within: 'Come in'.

Anuj pushes the door open and enters, exchanges pleasantries and takes a seat opposite

Mr Saxena.

Mr Saxena says, 'We have got the project that was on the anvil. I take my hat off to you. You have done very well. It was not all plain sailing, but you kept at it and brought it off. With patience, persistence and perseverance, you made the grade. I have looked into the matter and found out that your due promotion has been offered to another employee – Manu Sharma'.

This makes Anuj's head swirl. He is taken aback by this statement. This is the unkindest cut of all.

Though I know Manu for more than ten years, I realise now that I do not know him at all. We were together in college. I have always described him as a smart hardworking man of integrity, but he has come out in his true colours. There is more to him than meets the eye. He has a jealous streak in him as we joined at the same level, but I took an early step on the steep ladder of success by dint of sheer hard work while he stayed at the bottom rung.

He further continues, 'You played your cards well. I offer you a double promotion with the designation of a senior project manager'.

Anuj jumps at the offer, thanks him for his time and consideration, and leaves the cabin with a spring in his step. He is in the seventh heaven and his eyes are almost teary with happiness. He leaves the office premises and heads for the parking lot. He turns on the engine and is en route to the hospital.

Through countless physiotherapy sessions, he witnesses dad's gradual improvement. Finally the day comes when dad walks independently. It is a moment of sheer joy. He has anticipated this often in his dreams, but now it is real.

He shoots dad two thumbs up and a winning smile. He communicates all the details to him and presses his hand harder.

Dad says, 'I am happy the way it panned out. You have gone all out to make this happen', and adds 'Life is not always cakes and ale'.

The sun slips over the horizon and disappears out of sight.

The last few weeks have been an unhealthy blend of good and bad. Today is a chance to begin again.